NEELUK

An Eskimo Boy in the Days of the Whaling Ships

Stories by Frances Kittredge
Illustrations by Howard "Weyahok" Rock

ALASKA NORTHWEST BOOKS™

In memory of the Kingikmiut of Wales, and their descendants in Wales, Nome, Anchorage, Eagle River, Buckland, or wherever they may be; and in memory of my grandparents, Ellen and William Thomas Lopp, and Frances Kittredge.
—Kathleen Lopp Smith

A portion of the Originating Editor's proceeds from sales of *Neeluk: An Eskimo Boy in the Days of the Whaling Ships* will benefit the Wales Health Clinic Project in Wales, Alaska, and the Howard Rock Scholarship Program, administered by The CIRI Foundation, 2600 Cordova Street, Suite 206, Anchorage, Alaska 99503. For donation information, call (907) 263-5582 or fax (907) 263-5588.

Library of Congress Cataloging-in-Publication Data
Kittredge, Frances.
    Neeluk, an Eskimo boy in the days of the whaling ships / stories by Frances
Kittredge ; illustrations by Howard "Weyahok" Rock.
      p. cm.
      Summary: Traces the life of Neeluk and his family through one year in the
      1880s in the Arctic land that would later become the state of Alaska.
      ISBN 0-88240-545-4 (alk. paper) – ISBN 0-88240-546-2 (softbound : alk. paper)
    1. Eskimos—Juvenile fiction. [1. Eskimos—Fiction. 2. Alaska—Fiction.] I. Rock, Howard, ill. II. Title.

PZ7.K67165 Ne 2001
[Fic]—dc21   00-045371

Originating Editor: Kathleen Lopp Smith
Project Editor: Tricia Brown
Editor: Linda Gunnarson
Designer: Paulette Livers Lambert
Mapmaker: Gray Mouse Graphics
Cover illustration (inset): Howard "Weyahok" Rock
Cover map: Prepared for U.S. Bureau of Education by the U.S. Coast and Geodetic Survey to accompany Reindeer Report by
    Sheldon Jackson, D.D., U.S. General Agent of Education in Alaska, 1894

President/Publisher: Charles M. Hopkins
Editorial Staff: Douglas A. Pfeiffer, Ellen Harkins Wheat, Timothy W. Frew, Tricia Brown, Jean Andrews, Kathy Matthews,
    Jean Bond-Slaughter
Production Staff: Richard L. Owsiany, Susan Dupere

Alaska Northwest Books™ • An imprint of Graphic Arts Center Publishing Company
P.O. Box 10306, Portland, OR 97296-0306 • 503/226-2402 • www.gacpc.com
Printed on acid- and chlorine-free paper in Singapore

Acknowledgments

For their continued, enthusiastic encouragement for my projects related to the Lopp family in Alaska, I thank Jean and Robert Poulin, Mary and Roy Bordner, Margie and Rick Anderson, Gordon and Irene Dick, Tom G. Lopp, Catharine Kittredge Ford, and Diana Kronquist Johnson and family. I also thank my aunt, Weyana Lopp Schaal, who was born in Wales in 1899, for her interest in this book. Thanks also to Doris and Reub Klammer, Ann and Dick Stemwell, and Don and Joan Lopp. Special thanks to the individuals in Nome and Wales who proofread the book for cultural and historical accuracy: Vera Metcalf, Winton Weyapuk Jr., and Toby and Emma Anungazuk.

—Kathleen Lopp Smith

CONTENTS

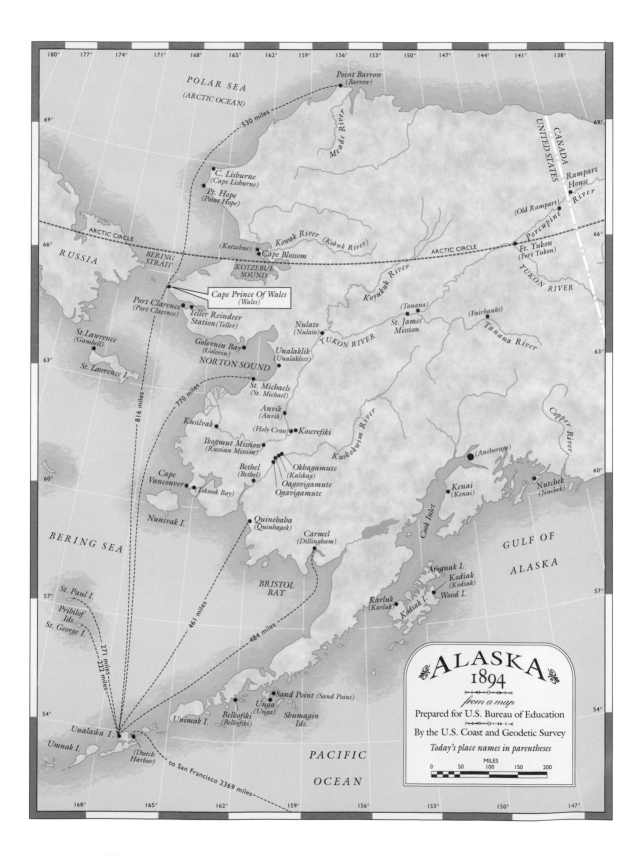

POLAR SEA
(ARCTIC OCEAN)

RUSSIA

BERING STRAIT

ARCTIC CIRCLE

Point Barrow
(Barrow)

530 miles

Meade River

UNITED STATES
CANADA

Rampart House

Porcupine River

(Old Rampart)

C. Lisburne
(Cape Lisburne)

Pt. Hope
(Point Hope)

Kowak River (Kobuk River)

(Kotzebue)   Cape Blossom

KOTZEBUE SOUND

ARCTIC CIRCLE

Ft. Yukon
(Fort Yukon)

YUKON RIVER

Koyukuk River

Cape Prince Of Wales
(Wales)

Port Clarence
(Port Clarence)

Teller Reindeer
Station (Teller)

Nulato
(Nulato)

YUKON RIVER

St. James
Mission

(Tanana)

(Fairbanks)

Tanana River

Golovnin Bay
(Golovin)

NORTON SOUND

Unalaklik
(Unalakleet)

St. Lawrence
(Gambell)

St. Lawrence I.

St. Michaels
(St. Michael)

Anvik
(Anvik)

(Holy Cross)   Koserefski

Kusilvak

816 miles

770 miles

Ikogmut Mission
(Russian Mission)

Bethel
(Bethel)

Okhagamute
(Kalskag)

Oagovigamute

Ogavigamute

Kuskokwim River

Copper River

(Anchorage)

Kenai
(Kenai)

Nutchek
(Nuchek)

Cape
Vancouver

(Toksook Bay)

Nunivak I.

Quinehaha
(Quinhagek)

Carmel
(Dillingham)

Cook Inlet

GULF OF
ALASKA

BERING SEA

BRISTOL
BAY

Afognak I.

Kodiak
(Kodiak)

Karluk
(Karluk)

Kodiak I.   Wood I.

St. Paul I.

Pribilof
Ids.

St. George I.

461 miles

484 miles

271 miles

222 miles

Unalaska I.

Umnak I.

(Dutch
Harbor)

to San Francisco 2369 miles

Unimak I.

Belkofski
(Belkofski)

Unga
(Unga)

Sand Point (Sand Point)

Shumagin
Ids.

PACIFIC

OCEAN

ALASKA
1894
from a map
Prepared for U.S. Bureau of Education
By the U.S. Coast and Geodetic Survey

Today's place names in parentheses

MILES
0   50   100   150   200

The Creation of **Neeluk**

In far northwestern Alaska, on a spit of land closer to Siberia than to any-where else on the North American continent, lies the tiny village of Wales. From this spot, the Russian mainland is less than sixty miles across the Bering Strait, so close that it takes little imagination to see how the Bering Land Bridge, now submerged, once connected two continents.

Inupiat Eskimo people have lived in this windy, treeless region for centuries, surviving long, harsh winters and brief summers through intimate knowledge of animal behavior and seasons, through inventive thinking, interdependence, and sharing.

Minnesota native Frances Kittredge arrived in Wales in 1900, when she was twenty-six years old. She came north for two years, joining her sister and brother-in-law, Ellen and William Thomas "Tom" Lopp, teachers for the U.S. Bureau of Education who were among the first non-Natives to settle in Wales.

When Frances arrived, the Lopps had already been living in the Arctic for almost ten years, and five of their eight children had been born there. The Lopps had been sent to teach the Natives; however, they also learned much from them. Over the years, Ellen and Tom learned how to speak Inupiaq, how to fish through the ice, how to dry a polar-bear hide, and how to "read" the sea ice and cross it safely. In the two years that Frances lived with the Lopps, she helped with child care and teaching. She also took special interest in local customs, especially how the villagers' work habits, and their children's play, changed with the seasons. Frances took notes as she talked with the people about their way of life, hoping to write about it someday.

In the late 1930s, after Tom and Ellen Lopp retired to Seattle, Frances asked them to review the manuscript that she had finally written—a simple story illustrating everyday life in Wales, month by month, as seen through the eyes of a fictional Inupiat child named Neeluk. She borrowed the name "Neeluk" from a valley located northeast of Wales, where villagers have always gathered wild onions, sourdock, and other greens. The stories began in July, Frances wrote in her original introduction, because it was "the warming-up time when flowers bloom and Eskimos go on trips for trading and fishing." The climax of the year came in April, May, and June, she wrote, "with whale and walrus hunting and the coming of whaling ships."

"It is with the knowledge gained from Tom and Ellen Lopp, even more than from personal experiences, that I was able to make these stories a real picture of Eskimo life at the time they represent," Frances wrote in 1939. "Tom Lopp has reviewed these stories, so that you may be sure they are in every way true to life."

The ways of the Eskimo were quite familiar to Alaskan illustrator Howard Rock, an Inupiat man from Point Hope, a village even farther north than Wales. At his birth, a shaman predicted that while the baby might never be a great hunter, nonetheless he would one day be a great man. In 1939, Howard was living with Tom and Ellen Lopp in Seattle while attending the University of Washington as an art student. In the Lopp home, he met Frances Kittredge, who commissioned the young man to paint and sketch a series of culturally and historically accurate illustrations for her story collection. He signed the paintings with his family name, *Weyahok,* which means "rock" in Inupiaq.

Frances Kittredge, 1902
Courtesy Lopp Smith Collection

Howard Rock's budding career as an artist would continue to flower as his work captured media attention and was shown throughout the Pacific Northwest. In short order, his paintings, sculptures, and pencil sketches achieved "collectible" status. Howard would also lend a hand to other rural Alaskan artists when he helped to found the Institute of Alaska Native Arts in the mid-1970s. But aside from the art world, he would make his mark in other ways, too. Howard became a respected advocate on behalf of his people in the late 1950s, when the government was proposing to use an atomic blast to excavate a harbor near Point Hope. He was called into leadership again when Natives around the state debated the terms of the Alaska Native Claims Settlement Act of 1971. He continued his work on behalf of Alaska Natives when he later founded a pioneering newspaper in Fairbanks titled *The Tundra Times,* in which all Natives found a voice. In 1974, Howard was awarded an honorary Doctor of Humane Letters degree from the University of Alaska Fairbanks, and a year later, *The Tundra Times* was nominated for a Pulitzer Prize. As foretold by the shaman in 1911, Weyahok had become a great man.

William Thomas (Tom) Lopp, 1902
Courtesy Lopp Smith Collection

The "days of the whaling ships" ended not long before the year 1900, when Frances Kittredge began living in Wales. Before the tall-masted whaling ships began sailing through the Bering Strait in the mid-1800s, the villagers knew and cared little for what was happening elsewhere. Adults were preoccupied with the immediate need for hunting and storing food and preparing for the coldest months. Villagers here and elsewhere in the Arctic hunted polar bears, caribou, walrus, and seals, but not only for the nourishing meat. Marine mammal skins would stretch over a driftwood frame to make a boat; reindeer hides covered a summer tent or made a soft bed or warm clothes; rendered blubber was a calorie-rich dip for meat or fish, a fuel source for cooking and heating. The animals and the land itself provided all of the raw materials that the villagers needed to make sleds, nets, drums, fishing floats, hooks, toys, tents, needles, and rope.

In *Neeluk: An Eskimo Boy in the Days of the Whaling Ships*, the Natives of Wales look for the first ship of the year with anticipation, ready to barter their trade goods for items such as guns and ammunition, caps and other American clothes, bolts of cloth and needles and thread. It may sound like a romantic time, when trade was conducted honorably. In truth, most whalers were disgraceful men who exploited whales and people to make a select few rich. By the late 1840s, up to three hundred New England whalers were slaughtering whales illegally in the waters surrounding Alaska, which at that time still belonged to the Russian empire. The American captains were reputed to be so cruel that no decent seaman would sign on voluntarily. Instead, crews were made up of victims: kidnapped American farm boys, newly arrived immigrants, or men who were taken from South Pacific ports as the ships sailed around Cape Horn.

Howard "Weyahok" Rock, ca. 1936
Courtesy Lopp Smith Collection

As for relations with Alaska Natives, the whalers' attitudes changed with time. In *Art and Eskimo Power,* a biography of Howard Rock, author Lael Morgan wrote: "Initially whalers feared the Eskimos and, although the Siberians soon ceased to be a threat, American Natives remained hostile well into the 1880s." The true stories of trade and the exploitation of Alaska's Natives are shameful, particularly following the introduction of whiskey.

9

Neeluk's stories, however, are those of an innocent, a little boy who is thrilled when his father returns from the whaling ship with gifts for the family. The stories may reflect a brief period when a measure of trust existed between villagers and whalers. But most importantly, they depict an age before the presence of foreigners—explorers, whalers, missionaries, government agents, and settlers—changed forever how Alaska Natives provided for and perceived themselves.

The Neeluk stories and illustrations capture a moment in Eskimo time and record the joys and struggles of subsisting in the High Arctic. To the Natives of Wales today, they are valued as echoes of oral histories that were lost in 1918, when the worldwide Spanish influenza epidemic swept across Alaska, taking the lives of so many elders who held a wealth of traditional knowledge.

Frances Kittredge died in 1940, leaving her unpublished Neeluk stories and the Howard Rock paintings to family members, who tucked them away for safekeeping for several decades. A champion for his people to his last day, Howard Rock passed away in April 1976. By the end of his life, his paintings, sculptures, and sketches had rocketed in value; yet his contributions as a Native leader and journalist may have been of greater consequence during a time of tremendous social and political change.

During the 1980s, a granddaughter of Tom and Ellen Lopp—Kathleen Lopp Smith—received the Lopp and Kittredge Alaska archives from various family elders. She learned how to use a computer so she could transcribe and compile the letters, journals, and stories of her grandmother, as well as those of her great-aunt, Frances Kittredge. Native friends and Alaska historians urged her to publish her family's papers and the Neeluk stories. With assistance from many other members of the Lopp-Kittredge family, these Neeluk stories and Howard Rock paintings will be published at last. It is with pride and pleasure that we at Alaska Northwest Books™ share them with you.

—*Tricia Brown*
Project Editor
May 2001

JULY

The boys dug as fast as they could.

The Boys' Lost River

One sunny July morning in the Inupiat Eskimo village of Wales, Alaska, a boy named Neeluk (KNEE-luck) had been playing games on the beach with many of the other boys and girls. The merry shouts of laughter had rung up and down the sandy shore. When the last big game ended, some of the children went home; the others divided into small groups. Seven-year-old Neeluk started walking up the beach with his cousin Wemok (WEE-muk) and two other boys who were their special friends, Keok (KEE-ok) and Ootenna (oo-TEN-ah).

The boys passed several girls seated in a circle in the sand. One of them was Konok (KAH-nuk), Neeluk's nine-year-old sister; another was Weeana (wee-AH-na), Wemok's sister, who was ten. The girls were playing a game much like ring-toss, using a short, slender stick in the center of the circle.

"Come and see us toss our bracelets," called Weeana.

The boys stopped beside them. The girls had taken off all their pretty bracelets and were trying to toss them in turn over the stick.

"You have done well, Weeana. You have tossed seven bracelets on the stick," said Neeluk. "Konok is a good tosser, too."

As the boys continued on their way, Wemok said, "The snow is almost gone, and the shore ice has drifted out to sea. I like to have it warm."

"I like to have it light all day and all night, too," said Ootenna. "Now we can play outdoors all the time."

On these long Arctic days, the Inupiat Eskimo children played as long as they could stay awake. Then they went home and slept a long, long time. Sometimes a boy would be having such a good time playing that, before he knew he was so tired, he would go to sleep right where he was. And there on the ground, or on the ice, he would sleep and sleep and sleep, unless someone picked him up and carried him home.

As the boys walked up the beach in search of new fun, they stopped now and then to watch the fast-moving little streams running across the sand. There had not been any the day before.

"See all the little rivers in the sand!" exclaimed Neeluk. Many tiny streams of water were cutting their way through the sand to the sea.

"What makes them?" asked Ootenna.

"They come from the hills, where the snow is melting," Keok answered, "and run out between the sand dunes onto the beach."

"Look!" exclaimed Neeluk. "Here are four little rivers close together! Let's make them all into one big, deep river. This is the largest one. I will dig it deeper with my stick and you boys can make the others run into it."

"I will make this river run into it," said Keok, beginning to dig a path in the sand through which to turn the nearest stream into Neeluk's.

"And I," said Ootenna, going to the stream farthest away, "will make this little river run into our big river."

The boys dug as fast as they could. Soon Keok called, "My stream runs into the big river!"

"Yours was the nearest," Wemok told him. "Come and help me dig."

The two boys worked together, and soon Wemok cried, "Now my stream runs into the big river!"

"Mine was the farthest away," said Ootenna. "Both you boys help me now."

So the three boys worked together till Ootenna shouted, "My stream runs into our big river!"

"Yes," said Neeluk. "Now all you boys help me dig the riverbed deeper so that the water will not run all over the sand." So the four boys worked together till they had a fine big river running all the way to the sea. The boys called their river a *kuuk,* which is the Inupiat Eskimo word for "river."

"Let's put fish in our river," said Neeluk. "Pieces of moss will be our fish. We will see who can spear the most."

"I will go," said Keok, "and pull some moss from the tundra."

"Don't get pieces that are too big—they will be too easy to spear," said Neeluk. Then the boys went home for their spears.

When they came back, they took turns, one of them staying at the head of the river and dropping in moss for fish, while the other three tried to spear them as they drifted swiftly by. They played a long time. Neeluk felt very good because he had succeeded in spearing more fish than Keok, who usually speared the most.

"I am going home now," Neeluk told the other boys. "I am hungry. Mother will have some walrus meat cooked."

"Oh, don't go!" begged the other boys. "Play a little longer."

"But I am sleepy, too," said Neeluk. "I have been awake this whole long day."

Bead bracelet

"Please stay a little longer and play with us," coaxed Wemok. "Then I will go with you." Keok had caught more fish than Wemok, and Wemok wanted to catch up with him.

"I will play a little longer," Neeluk said. It was his turn to drop in fish, so he dropped in a fish, then another and another.

"I've speared a big one!" shouted Wemok. He waited for the next fish, but none came.

"Put in more fish!" Wemok called to Neeluk, keeping his eyes on the water. But still none came. He called again.

"Neeluk has gone to sleep," said Ootenna. "I will throw a wet fish across his face." But Neeluk was sleeping too soundly to feel it.

"Wake up!" shouted Wemok, shaking him. But Neeluk did not wake up.

"Wake up! shouted Keok, poking him. "If you sleep, your folks will eat all the walrus meat!" But Neeluk slept right on.

"Here comes his father," said Ootenna, and the boys stopped teasing him.

"What are you doing to Neeluk?" asked his father.

"He went to sleep," said Wemok, "and we are trying to wake him up."

"Let him sleep," said his father. "He has been awake since midday yesterday." He stooped and, lifting the sleeping boy, carried him home. The other boys followed in single file.

"We will come back and fish tomorrow," Wemok said.

"Yes," agreed Keok, "we will come as soon as we wake up." They did not know what would happen to their river in the night.

Neeluk's friends followed Neeluk's father up from the beach and along the path that lay between the double row of summer tents and igloos, or *innis*, as they called them. The igloos were winter houses, built partially underground for better shelter. But in summer, the villagers lived in tents of walrus hide supported by pieces of driftwood. Each boy went to his own tent.

Neeluk had been right when he said his mother would have walrus meat cooked. It had boiled long enough, and she had taken the meat from the kettle and put it in a large wooden dish. She cut it up in small pieces. Grandfather, Grandmother, and Konok were already seated on the ground. Neeluk's mother set the dish of walrus meat in front of them. She took the kettle of broth from the fire and set it beside the dish of meat. She brought several ladles, carved from driftwood, from which to drink the broth. She brought one thing more: a little wooden bowl of seal oil, for the villagers liked to eat a little seal oil with their meat. Now dinner was ready. This was all there was to eat, for in those days the people had no bread and butter, no vegetables, no canned foods. Meat and fish were almost all they had year round. Sometimes they could enjoy freshly picked berries; other times, their meals included greens that had been gathered in summer, stored in seal oil in skin bags, and eaten in winter.

Just as everything was ready, Neeluk's father came home carrying Neeluk. Everyone was disappointed that Neeluk was asleep and would miss his dinner.

Eskimo clay kettle

"Can't you wake him?" asked Grandmother.

So Neeluk's father shook him and shouted, "Wake up! Wake up, Neeluk, and eat!"

But Neeluk did not hear. So Neeluk's father took him into the tent and laid him on some reindeer-skin robes. Then the family ate. As for Neeluk, he had been awake for so long that he would probably sleep for as long as fifteen hours. But his mother would save some of the meat for him for when he woke up.

That night Neeluk and the other boys slept so soundly that they did not hear the great wind that blew up from the south. Keok was the first to wake. The sun was shining warmly. It was already the middle of the next day. He went to Ootenna's tent and woke him, and the two boys hurried to their river on the beach.

It was gone! The boys stared in amazement. There was not a sign of it. Where the river had been, the sand was leveled as smooth as the rest of the beach.

"I will tell Neeluk!" exclaimed Ootenna. He ran to the tent where Neeluk was still sleeping and burst in shouting, "Neeluk! Come quick! Our river is gone! The wind has blown it away!"

Half awake, Neeluk sprang to his feet and ran after Ootenna to where the river had been. He gazed at the smooth sand. He was disappointed. Keok had gone to where the four little rivers had come out between the sand dunes. Three girls were coming down the tundra in back of the sand dunes. One of the girls was Keok's sister, Woodluk, who was twelve. They stopped when they reached the boys.

"We have been looking for flowers," Woodluk said as she and the other girls showed the bright, dainty little blossoms they had found. "These are the first flowers we have seen this summer."

Keok told about the river they had made. "I do not understand," he said, "how the wind could blow it full of sand when so much water was running in it."

"The wind did it in the night," said Woodluk, "when not much water was running because the sun was not very warm and the snow on the hills was not melting."

"We wanted to spear fish," said Neeluk.

"You can," Woodluk said, "because when it grew warmer today, and there was more water, it came out through a new place, a little farther up the beach, where drifted sand did not keep it back from the sea. You boys can play there."

Away the boys ran up the beach. They had gone not more than two hundred steps when they came to such a fine stream of water cutting its way through the sand to the sea that Ootenna exclaimed, "It is better than our river!"

"It is wider and deeper," said Keok.

"And we can spear fish in it," said Neeluk. "I will go and wake up Wemok and get my spear while you boys pull moss for fish. Then we will see who can spear the most."

Spear

18

AUGUST

"If you will give me your cap, you can take him."

Neeluk and the Eskimo Puppy

Konok! Neeluk! Wake up!" called their mother early one August morning. "The wind has changed, and we are going to start to Kotzebue as soon as we can get ready!" They were going to Kotzebue Sound with many other families to catch and dry big salmon to eat in winter. For a week, Neeluk and Konok had been eagerly waiting for the wind to change so it would be safe to set out in their boats.

The children were hardly out of bed before their mother was rolling up the reindeer skins in which they had slept and their father was taking off the walrus-skin covering of their summer tent. They would need them at Kotzebue. Grandmother was packing the kettle, a few wooden dishes, and other things they would need there. Grandfather was in the driftwood igloo, where they lived in the winter, getting out the furs and other goods he was going to trade to the people at Kotzebue.

You may be sure Neeluk did not forget to put on the new blue-cloth cap with a visor that his grandfather had bought for him on the whaling ship that spring. He was the only one of the younger boys in the village who had a cap. A few of the older boys had them, and so did many of the men. His people had just lately begun to buy caps on whaling ships. Before that they had worn only their hoods and, when the hoods were too warm, had pushed them back and gone bare-headed. They all wanted to trade for caps, but the caps cost so much in trade goods that they had to buy things they needed more instead. Neeluk's grandfather had paid a white fox skin for Neeluk's cap.

Soon all who were going to Kotzebue Sound were on the beach. The grown folks were packing their luggage in *umiaks,* great skin boats that were deep and wide and forty feet long. Neeluk and Konok and their cousins—Wemok and his sister, Weeana, and four-year-old brother Ahlook—were all going in the same boat.

The weather was clear, and the wind filled their big, square sails made of canvas. They traveled day and night, as it was light all the

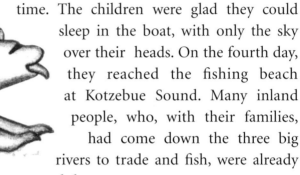

time. The children were glad they could sleep in the boat, with only the sky over their heads. On the fourth day, they reached the fishing beach at Kotzebue Sound. Many inland people, who, with their families, had come down the three big rivers to trade and fish, were already camped there.

Small, carved ivory dog

The next morning Neeluk watched his grandfather trading with the men from up the rivers. He watched carefully, for he hoped to be a good trader when he grew up. Some boys had come with the men. One of them, a boy almost twice as old as Neeluk and whose name was Topkok, talked about four little puppies he had. When Topkok went to his tent, Neeluk and Wemok and some bigger boys went with him to see them. They were fine little iron-gray pups. Neeluk thought the one with white on the tip of its nose and the tip of its tail was the best puppy he had ever seen. Neeluk liked him so much that the next morning he followed some big boys to Topkok's tent so he could see the puppy again. The puppy liked Neeluk, too.

The next day Neeluk took his grandfather to see the puppy. Neeluk's grandfather was very good to his grandson, so Neeluk hoped he would buy the puppy for him with trade goods. He was pleased when Grandfather said it was a fine pup.

When Neeluk saw Topkok again, he asked him what he would trade the puppy for. "I will trade him for your cap," Topkok answered without hesitation.

Neeluk was so surprised at the very idea of trading his precious cap that he put his hand up to it as if he thought the cap, which was a little large, might get away from him. "I would not trade this cap that Grandfather gave me," he said, "but Grandfather has other trade goods from the whalers: powder and shot, knives, cloth, and other things. I will ask him to trade you what you want for the puppy."

"I won't trade him for anything except your cap," replied Topkok. "I like that puppy, too. For your cap I will trade him, but not for anything else."

Neeluk went home disappointed. He told his grand-father about what Topkok had said, hoping he would make such a good offer for the puppy that Topkok would take it. But Grandfather only smiled and said, "The cap is yours, Neeluk. If you want to trade it for the puppy, you may. It is a promising pup. It will be a good trade."

Small, carved ivory dog

Neeluk told his mother about it. "Neeluk," she said, "do you not want to be a great trader like your grandfather? Then you must think what this trade may mean. You like the cap, but you do not need it, and it will soon be old. The puppy may become a sled dog that will give you ten years of service."

"But I like my cap," said Neeluk. "I do not want to trade it. I wish Topkok would trade the puppy for some of Grandfather's trade goods."

The days went by. Neeluk often went and played with the puppy. Sometimes, when he started home, the puppy followed him. Then Neeluk had to make him go back. Sometimes he had to carry him back. How Neeluk wished Topkok would sell the puppy for trade goods! Then the puppy could follow him to his tent, and he could keep him all the time. But Neeluk knew from the longing way that Topkok sometimes looked at his cap that he would not trade for anything else.

At last it was time to go home. The next morning they would start. Neeluk went to see the puppy for the last time. Topkok saw how much Neeluk wanted him. "If you will give me your cap," he said, "you can take him."

When it was time for Neeluk to leave, the puppy followed him. What a fine puppy he was! And how pretty! His white-tipped tail, curled up over his back, matched the white tip on his pointed nose. Neeluk told the puppy to go back, but he would not go. Neeluk had to take him up in his arms and carry him back. He had no more than set the puppy down when it started following him again. Topkok was watching them. Neeluk looked longingly at the puppy. How could he take him back again? Slowly his hand went up to his cap. Slowly he took it off and gave it to Topkok.

"Now the puppy may follow me," Neeluk said.

Bare-headed, but with the puppy, Neeluk entered his family's camp. His grandfather saw him and looked pleased. "I see you have made your first trade, Neeluk," he said.

His father smiled and said, "He is a good puppy. Someday you will be driving him."

His mother was pleased, too. "You have done well, Neeluk," she said. "It is wise to trade that which one does not need for something useful. Someday you will be as good a trader as your grandfather."

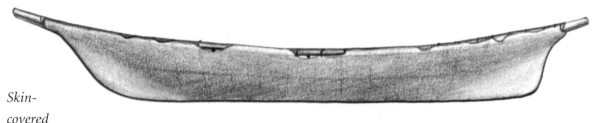

*Skin-
covered
boat*

24

SEPTEMBER

The seven fish hung down from the thong like great beads.

Boot Tops from the Sea

One September afternoon Neeluk and his cousin Wemok donned their waterproof boots to wade in the shallow water at the edge of the beach. The boys' boots were made of tanned sealskin, and their mothers had sewn them with waterproof stitches. The boys liked to feel the little waves breaking around their feet.

Neeluk's pup, which he had named Ogluk (OG-luck), was watching them. The puppy looked very cute with his little white-tipped nose and his white-tipped tail curled up over his back. He played in the surf while the boys waded.

"I like to wear waterproof boots," said Wemok.

"Yes. They are nice to wear in summer," said Neeluk, "but when winter comes we will need warmer ones—fur boots."

"I haven't any warmer boots," Wemok replied. "My fawn-skin boots are too small, and my sealskin boots are almost worn out. Mother is going to make me some new boots when Father catches another seal."

"If he does not catch one soon," said Neeluk, "our feet will get cold. Winter is coming."

In those long-ago days, the people looked to the sea for most of what they ate and wore.

"Look," cried Wemok, "there goes Father! He is going to look at his fish net." His father was wearing his waterproof *atigi*, which was like a raincoat, and carrying his kayak to the water's edge.

The fish net looked something like a tennis net, only its meshes were larger and made of sealskin thong, or string. It was a hundred and fifty feet long and stretched right out into the ocean. The fish that swam along near

Carved ivory seals

the shore would find a net stretched across their way. When they swam against it and tried to get through by jamming their heads through its meshes, they could get no farther. The more they struggled, the more they became entangled.

"I hope, Father, that you will find many fish in the net today," Wemok said as he and Neeluk caught up with him.

"Yes," his father answered, "we need them very much."

The boys watched Wemok's father get into the kayak. He tied the bottom of his waterproof *atigi* around the rim of the round hole of the kayak so that no water could get in. Then he started paddling out beside the net.

Wemok liked fish boiled, and he liked them dried. But there never were as many boiled or dried fish as were needed. Meat and fish were almost everything the Eskimo people had to eat.

The boys saw Wemok's father stop and take the first fish from the net. He strung it on a piece of sealskin thong, which hung around his neck, and went on. He stopped again.

"Now he has found another fish!" cried Wemok.

After the second fish had been strung on the thong, Wemok's father paddled on and then stopped.

"He has found another fish!" Wemok cried again.

"Two of them!" exclaimed Neeluk.

"And another!" said Wemok.

They watched him take out a sixth fish and then go on. He was nearly to the end of the net when he stopped again and took out the last fish.

"Seven fish!" exclaimed the boys.

When Wemok's father had strung the last fish on the sealskin string and tied the ends of the string together, he did not start to paddle back. Instead, he reached low in the water, the kayak tipping far to one side.

"What is he doing?" asked Wemok excitedly. Then the boys saw him reaching down to something beneath the water. Then he leaned again.

"Look," cried Wemok delightedly, "he has found a seal caught in the net! It drowned because it could not come up to the surface for air."

When Wemok's father got the hair seal free from the torn net, he tied a thong to it and fastened it behind the kayak.

"See, now he is towing the seal to shore," said Neeluk.

Wemok's father looked pleased. The seven fish, each about a foot long, hung down from the thong like great beads on a necklace. The boys were happy, too. "Now your mother will be able to make you some new boots," Neeluk said.

Soon Wemok's father reached shore and pulled himself out of the kayak. The boys admired the seal. It was three feet long and weighed about fifty pounds. Wemok's father took a strap from the kayak and put it about his shoulders, harness-like. He tied the end of it to the strap by which the seal had been towed. He had taken off the string of fish and given it to the boys to hold.

High-topped boots

"I will drag the seal home," he told the boys, "and then come back for the fish and kayak." Then he added, jokingly, "Don't let your puppy eat the fish, Neeluk."

The boys were so interested in watching Wemok's father drag the seal home, and in talking about what fine boot tops the seal's skin would make, that the first thing they knew, they felt a hard pull on the string of fish. They looked around quickly and there was the puppy, trying to get one of the precious fish.

"Let go! Let go!" the boys shouted, shooing Ogluk away. It wasn't long before Wemok's father returned for the fish and kayak. As he turned for home, the boys followed, and the puppy danced behind them.

Wemok sought out his mother as soon as he entered the tent.

"It is a good skin for my boot tops, isn't it, Mother?" he asked eagerly.

"Yes," she answered, "and I will make your boots as soon as the skin is dry." Then she said to Neeluk, "Go home and tell your mother to come with a dish and get a piece of seal meat for supper."

Neeluk went quickly. Seal meat tasted good, and he had not had any for a long time. His mother was glad, too. So were his sister, Konok, and Wemok's sister, Weeana, who was playing with her.

"We are going back with you," said the girls.

"I want to see how big the seal is," said Weeana.

"I want to see it cut up," said Konok.

When they reached Wemok's tent, they saw that Wemok's mother had skinned the seal and was cutting it up.

Soon Konok and Neeluk and their mother were on their way home, all rejoicing over the fine piece of seal meat Mother was carrying in her wooden dish.

"What would we do without seals?" asked Neeluk. "We eat their meat, and we eat the oil from their fat with meat and with dried fish."

"And we make boots and trousers and belts from their skins," added Konok, "and nets to catch fish."

"And we use their skins for bags," said Neeluk, "and for buoys when they are blown full of air."

"We couldn't get along without seals, could we, Mother?" Konok asked.

"No," she answered, "we could not live without them."

Then they reached home, and Mother soon had the seal meat boiling over a driftwood fire.

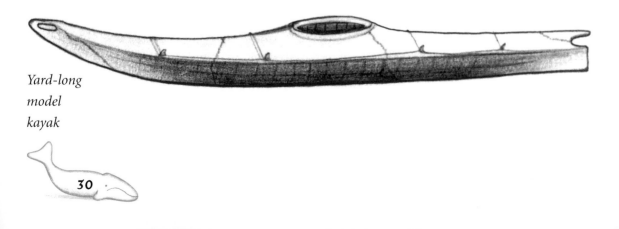

Yard-long model kayak

OCTOBER

She fastened the belt that kept him snug.

The Lost Needle

It was October. The winds were cold, and often it snowed. The people of Wales had moved from their summer tents into their snug winter *innis*. October was the busiest sewing month of all the year, for everybody needed something new. Neeluk needed a new *atigi*—a hooded, fur shirt that you pull on over your head.

One day when Neeluk went to the beach to play with some friends, he said to his cousin Wemok, "Mother is making me a new *atigi*. It is going to be very good and warm. In a while I must go home and try it on."

"My mother is going to make me an *atigi*, too," said Wemok, "as soon as she finishes Father's."

"Yes, and my mother is going to make me some sealskin trousers," added Ootenna.

Konok and Weeana and some other girls stopped to talk with them.

"How many things our mothers sew!" exclaimed Weeana. "They make all our *atigis* and trousers."

"They make fur boots and socks," said Keok.

"And belts," Wemok added.

"They make gloves," Keok said, "and mittens."

"And," said Neeluk, "they sew walrus skins together for boats."

"They make sails for our little boats, too," said Konok.

"And balls for us to play with," added Wemok.

"I am glad," said Weeana, "that the men on whaling ships trade us needles to sew with. It would be hard to sew so many things with bone needles, as Grandmother says they used to."

It was too cold on the beach to stand and talk. Soon the girls were playing a game like "hopscotch," and the boys were running races, with a drift log for their goal.

When Neeluk thought it was time to go home and try on his new *atigi,* Wemok, Keok, and Ootenna went with him to see it.

When they came to Neeluk's *inni,* you would hardly have known that it was a house. It was built, as the other village igloos were, of split drift logs and banked with sod and sand to keep out the wind. The window was in the roof. The doorway, a hole two feet square that was over the outer end of the long hall, was in the roof, too, and had a rim around it to hold onto when dropping down or climbing out.

The boys dropped through this hole in the roof onto a platform three feet below. From this platform they went down a ladder to the hall floor, which was five feet lower.

"It takes longer to get into our igloos than into our tents," said Ootenna.

"Yes," said Neeluk, "but we need these long passages to keep the wind and cold out of our igloo." They ran through the long, twelve-foot passageway to the little doorway of the room in which the whole family lived. The floor of this room was more than a foot higher than that of the passageway. It was a climb for small boys to get up into the room.

"Up we go," said Neeluk. He pushed back the skin curtain that was used for a door and crawled in. The other boys quickly followed. The doorway was just high enough and wide enough for a man to crawl through. It was made small to keep out the cold. Years later, when white people came, they often found it difficult to get in through these little doorways.

The room was about fifteen feet square. It was well lit by the overhead skylight made of thin, waterproof seal gut. The logs used for making the inner wall of the igloo had been split, and the smooth split side faced inside.

Neeluk's mother and grandmother sat sewing beside one of the two flat, tray-like lamps that were burning. These lamps were filled with oil and had moss for wicks. Pieces of blubber hung above the lamps. The heat from the lamps made drops of oil fall from the blubber, keeping the lamps supplied with oil. In such a cold country, where winters were so long, the people used these stone lamps to cook and to keep warm.

Another woman had come to visit. Her name was Kopkina (cop-KEE-na), and she had brought her baby with her. Kopkina had carried the baby on her back inside her *atigi* and had taken him out when she came into the igloo.

When the boys came crawling in, Grandmother said, "Pull the curtain down quickly, boys. You are bringing in much cold air. This is a cold day. We have stuffed the little hole in the ceiling with dried grass to keep us warmer." The boys made the curtain as tight as they could and glanced at the grass sticking out of the little hole high up.

Eskimo oil lamp

"Many boys have come to see Neeluk try on his new *atigi*!" Neeluk's mother exclaimed. She put it on over his head.

"*Aanikaa!*" the boys exclaimed, which meant, "How fine!" *Aanikaa* is an unusual Inupiaq word. If it is said in a pleasant way, it means "How good!" or "How fine!" If it is said in a sorry way, it means, "It is too bad." And if it is said in a sharp or gruff way, it means, "You're bad."

As the boys looked at the soft, brown fawn skin and the fur that was to trim the hood, they said, "*Aanikaa!*" again and again.

"But it does not fit right," said Neeluk's mother. "Wait, and I will change it."

While the boys waited, they played with the baby. He was a happy little fellow, about a year old, and laughed with delight as the boys romped on the floor with him.

Neeluk was still wearing the *atigi* while his mother cut a piece of fur to set in, then checked to be sure it was right. "Now it will fit well," she said. "You boys can go back and play on the beach."

Neeluk was slipping out of the *atigi* when he heard his mother saying in a surprised and sorry way, "*Aanikaa!* Where is my needle?"

*Needle
and
thread*

"It must be where you put it," Grandmother said, "when you cut that piece of fawn skin."

But it was not. Such hunting went on! Everyone hunted but the baby. How many times one or another said, *"Aanikaa!"* in a sorry way. Everyone hoped the needle had not gone down a crack in the floor, because if it had, they could never get it.

"Perhaps," Grandmother said, "the needle caught on the clothes of one of the boys when they were playing with the baby." The three women searched every inch of the boys' clothes but could not find it.

"Aanikaa!" exclaimed Neeluk's mother. "What shall I do if the needle has gone down a crack? It is only fall now, and I have not many needles to last till the ships come in the spring."

The women looked the boys over again, and Grandmother said, "You boys go outdoors and play now."

"I will go, too," said Kopkina. Then she picked up her baby to put him on her back, under her *atigi*. The *atigi* was made in a special way for carrying a baby. Still, it is quite a trick to put the baby up under it. With a quick, skillful movement she put the baby behind her, low down; then, holding him with both hands, she pushed him up under her *atigi* as far as she could reach. Next, she bent forward very low till her head was near the floor, shaking the baby toward her shoulders, while with both hands she pushed him forward. She was doing this as fast as she could, for it was rather a smothery place for the baby till his head could come out by his mother's. Suddenly Kopkina gave a cry of pain and straightened up. Mother and Grandmother sprang toward her. She let the baby fall from under her *atigi* into their hands.

"The needle!" Kopkina cried. "It's in the baby's clothes!"

And there it was. *"Aanikaa!"* everybody said with happy voices, so glad the needle was found. Kopkina put the baby on her back again, this time shaking him forward till his head came out over her left shoulder. She fastened the belt that kept him snug and comfortable. Then she said good-bye and backed out through the little doorway.

Mother and Grandmother smiled at each other before Mother returned to her sewing. Neeluk's *atigi* was nearly finished.

NOVEMBER

In an instant Ogluk was jerked off his feet and pulled over.

Neeluk and Ogluk
Learn to Be Careful

It was late November, and the nights had grown so long that there were only a few hours of light. One evening Neeluk and his sister, Konok, were very happy. They had just heard that there was to be a party the next night, and all the family were going. The party would be held at one of the *kazgis,* the large houses where villagers gathered to talk over community business, work together, or have parties. When they went to parties at the *kazgis,* they wore their best clothes.

"I am going to make Neeluk a new wolverine belt to wear to the party," Grandmother said. "His old one has too much fur worn off." Grandmother called the belt by its Inupiaq name: *tavsik.* She brought out some lovely pieces of soft, brown fur. They were cut from the legs of a wolverine skin and were thin and very strong. Wolverine skins made the best belts.

Neeluk was pleased. "Will you leave the claws on, Grandmother?" he asked. The claws were considered very ornamental.

"Yes," she answered.

"And I," said Grandfather, "will give Neeluk the ivory bear head that I am carving for his new belt fastener."

Part of the evening Neeluk watched Grandmother sewing together the little pieces of wolverine skin; but most of the time, he watched Grandfather finishing the ivory button he was carving in the shape of a bear's head. Grandfather cut fine lines to make the eyes, nose, and mouth. Then he rubbed soot from the bottom of a kettle into the lines till they were as black as if made with ink. He carved an opening through which the bear-head button could be sewed onto the belt.

That night it snowed and snowed, and the wind blew hard from the south. The wind swept most of the snow off the beach, drifting it around the igloos. The people liked this because it made their igloos warmer. The wind drifted the snow around the Eskimo dogs, too. The dogs liked it because it made them warmer where they lay in the snow. Few Eskimo dogs had any shelter. When night came, they would find the softest places they could in the snow and whirl around and around, hollowing out little places to lie in, with their tails covering their noses. There they would sleep all night, with the cold wind blowing over them. They liked to have the snow cover them, for it was like a blanket to keep them warm. On this night, the snow drifted over the dogs until only slight mounds showed where the dogs were sleeping.

Morning came, but not daylight. The storm had ceased. Father and Grandfather started off in the darkness to hunt seals. Mother and Grandmother sat on the floor on either side of the seal-oil lamp, sewing as fast as they could.

Bear-head button

"You will have a very good *tavsik*, Neeluk, to wear to the *kazgi*," Grand-mother told him.

Neeluk and Konok were playing with the little husky puppies. There were four of them, just old enough to be playful. They had been brought into the house because it was too cold for them to sleep out-of-doors. Konok and Neeluk were glad to have them in the house. As they played, the children watched carefully to be sure the puppies would not get hold of anything they could chew up. It would never do for the puppies to bite holes in their clothes or bedding.

Konok was playing with one of the puppies, just as she would have played with a large doll if she had had one. She was carrying the puppy on her back, much as her mother had her when she was a baby, fastening an upper and lower belt to keep the "baby" in place. Neeluk was having just as good a time with another of the puppies. He had hitched it to a very small, lightweight, bone sled and was trying to train it to pull the sled around the room.

At last a little daylight came down through the thin, skin skylight. Mother put away her sewing. "I am going for ice," she said. "Would you children like to go with me? That little piece is our last."

The children glanced toward the ice shelf. It was a hewn plank placed like a slanting shelf against the wall. It was set rather high so that the ice or snow placed at the top would get more heat and melt faster. There were grooves in the plank; as the snow or ice melted, their drinking and cooking water flowed down these grooves and into a pail at the lower end.

"Neeluk, I think your *tavsik* will be finished by the time you get back," Grandmother said.

The children were eager to go. First they had to fasten the puppies so they could not run around the living room. That was easily done, for the puppies wore little harnesses with two-foot-long pulling straps. At the end of each strap they tied a little stick, then they placed the sticks in cracks in the floor so that the puppies could not pull them out.

Neeluk and Konok put on their warm furs, fastened their belts, and followed their mother. Mother had taken five dog harnesses from the storeroom, and Konok and Neeluk followed her up out of the entrance.

"There are only four dogs," said Konok. "Where is the other?"

"You and Neeluk can hunt for him," Mother said, "while I harness these to the sled."

Where could the fifth dog be? Mother had the four others harnessed to the sled while Konok and Neeluk were looking everywhere.

"I think he is here!" cried Konok, pushing at a little mound of snow with the toe of her boot. Sure enough, there was Neeluk's dog, Ogluk, "as snug as a bug in a rug." Soon they were ready to start.

"May I be the one, Mother," Neeluk asked, "to run in front of the dogs and choose the way to go?" The storm had covered the path.

"Yes," his mother told him, "if you think you can choose a good way. Konok may ride on the sled."

Ogluk was in harness just in front of the sled. Perhaps someday he would be a leader, but as a young dog, he was still learning to work as a team member. Then they were off! The eager lead dog and the others sprang forward while Ogluk was still stretching his stiff muscles. In an instant Ogluk was jerked off his feet and pulled over.

Mother called to the leader to stop, and she stepped off the runners and pulled back on the handles to keep the sled from sliding onto Ogluk. Quickly Neeluk turned to see Ogluk struggle back to his feet. Mother was smiling. "Next time he will watch with both eyes and listen with both ears," she said, and off they went again. How the children liked it!

Neeluk was running fast as he could, and the leader dog kept close behind him. Mother was steadying the back of the sled and was running just as fast. They would cut the ice one-fourth of a mile up the river. They went so far because, near the village, salty sea water had mingled with the river water before freezing.

Ivory dog

Mother set right to work cutting out blocks of ice. She used an adz that Grandfather had bought for trade goods on a ship. The dogs lay down on the snow and waited. There wasn't much Neeluk and Konok could do to help, so they had fun sliding on the ice.

Meanwhile, alone except for Wemok and the four sleeping puppies, Grandmother sewed stitch after stitch on Neeluk's *tavsik*. Soon she decided to build a fire in the kitchen and start some walrus meat boiling so that there would be plenty to eat when the hunters and ice-gatherers came home. She would boil not only enough for the family, but some extra to take to the *kazgi*. She laid down Neeluk's belt and went to the kitchen. The puppies woke up and watched her go.

When Grandmother came back, the puppies were playing. She sat down to sew, but the belt was gone! Where could it be? No one had come in. Grandmother looked at the puppies.

"Drop it! Drop it!" she cried as she sprang toward the pups. They were playing with Neeluk's new *tavsik,* and it was a sorry sight.

Ivory dog

The belt was chewed and chewed, and in some places there were holes clear through. At first it looked too ruined to mend. How sad Neeluk would be! There were no other wolverine skin pieces that could be spared for another belt. Then, as Grandmother looked more carefully, she saw that if she cut out the most chewed places and set in new scraps matching them nicely, the belt would be almost as good as before. She set to work as fast as she could, but first she fastened the puppy whose stick had come out of its crack.

It took a long time for Neeluk's mother to cut enough ice, but at last it was done. Konok and Neeluk helped put it on the sled. When they reached home, they unloaded the ice close to the entrance of the house. They unharnessed the dogs and then lifted the sled to the top of the tall rack so that the hungry dogs would not eat the thong that tied the parts of the sled together. They tied the sled firmly to the rack so that the strong winds would not blow it off. Then they went into the igloo, with Mother carrying a piece of ice.

Neeluk went straight to where his grandmother was sewing, hoping the *tavsik* would be finished and ready to put on. Instead, it looked about as it had when he went away.

"You did not sew much on it while we were gone, did you, Grandmother?" he asked, disappointed.

"Yes," she answered, "I have sewed much on it. I stopped only to start the walrus meat cooking." Then she told him about the puppies and showed him the chewed pieces she had cut out of the belt and where she had set in the new pieces.

"It was one of the puppies you fastened that got loose, Neeluk." Grandmother spoke kindly, but Neeluk could see that she was very sorry that he had been so careless.

"Your grandfather is a very good hunter, Neeluk," she told him, "and he is a careful man. So is your father. If you are going to be a great hunter, Neeluk, you, too, must be very cautious.

"Remember this," she added. "A careful boy makes a careful man."

Neeluk was determined that he would be.

Then Grandmother smiled and said, "I will have the belt finished in time for you to wear it to the *kazgi*, Neeluk. It will not be long before you see me sewing on the bear-head button."

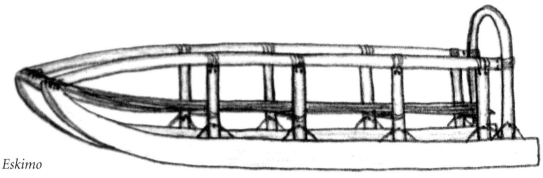

Eskimo sled

DECEMBER

The dog had grabbed the ball in his mouth.

A Surprise for Neeluk

It had been such a cold, cloudy December morning that the village boys and girls had stayed in their warm igloos. But in the late morning, when at last the sun showed itself, they took their balls and went out on the snow-covered beach to play. Their balls were large and stuffed with reindeer hair. They kicked them over the snow and, running after them, kicked them on again as far as they could. All over the beach in front of the village, children were running and kicking their balls, and many were running races with their friends. All too soon, twilight came, and the boys and girls started home.

"Come Neeluk!" called Konok.

"Keok and I want to run another race," Neeluk called back.

"All right," answered Konok, "we will watch and see who wins."

Other children who had started home turned to see the race. They were not the only ones who watched. Two dogs had come down to the beach and were looking on, but no one noticed them.

The race began. Up the beach, a drift log sticking up above the snow was the goal. Neeluk and Keok were running and kicking their balls as fast as they could. With so many watching, each felt he must win. Keok was the fastest runner, but there were so many little snow drifts that could send the balls going the wrong way that it took skill, too. First Neeluk was ahead, then Keok.

"Look out for the dogs!" shouted the boys and girls. But how could Neeluk and Keok, now so far away, and with all their attention on the race, hear what they said?

The boys were nearing the goal, with Keok's ball ahead; then Neeluk gave his ball a well-directed kick that sent it flying over so many little drifts and

Ivory dog

ridges that it landed on the snow beyond Keok's. He might win yet! Then, suddenly, out in front of the astonished Neeluk bounded a speeding dog, making straight for his ball! Before Neeluk could do anything to stop him, the dog had grabbed the ball in his mouth and was running away toward the village. Neeluk and Keok gave chase. The other children ran, too.

"Head him off!" "Stop him!" "Drop the ball!" The children ran and shouted, trying to rescue Neeluk's ball. But they could not head the dog off, for he turned and ran out over the ice. Soon Neeluk's good ball was torn open, with its reindeer-hair stuffing scattered over the ice.

"Never mind," Keok said, trying to cheer up his friend. "The dogs won that race." But Neeluk did mind.

Neeluk walked home slowly. The early supper was ready. There was boiled whale meat and broth. As soon as supper was over, he went to bed.

Neeluk did not have a bed with four legs, a mattress, a pillow, sheets, blankets, and a spread. The only bed in the igloo was a great big bunk, or sleeping shelf, four feet high, made of hewn planks. It was more than six feet from front to back and reached across the whole end of the room. Whoever did not sleep on the shelf slept on the floor beneath. Reindeer-skin robes were used for mattress and bedding.

Neeluk took off his boots and left them on the floor. At each end of the bunk there was a post with deep notches cut into it. Neeluk stepped onto the notches, like a ladder, to help him climb into his high bed. He pulled off all his clothes and, putting them under his head for a pillow, snuggled down between the fur sleeping robes. Soon he was asleep.

Konok climbed the ladder to make sure Neeluk was sound asleep. She smiled as she climbed down, for she had a happy idea. She said to her mother, "May I make a new ball for Neeluk? If you cut the pieces, I will sew them. I wish it could be finished tonight so Neeluk will see it as soon as he wakes up in the morning."

"Bring me the box of tanned sealskin pieces," Mother told her.

They were soft pieces—some dark brown, some light, and some that had been dyed red. First Konok's mother cut out two round pieces that would be the top and bottom caps of the ball. Then she cut out many little pieces of different shapes and colors that, when sewed together, would make a pretty design and a round ball.

Sitting on the floor beside her mother, Konok began sewing the pieces together with neat, strong stitches. Konok sewed steadily, but she found it was slow work taking stitches so carefully that the ball would be strong enough to kick around.

She soon knew she could not finish the ball herself that night and was glad when her mother began to help. Then Konok started to get sleepy. She grew sleepier every minute, but tried her best to keep sewing. How quickly her mother was sewing the pieces together! They would finish the ball that night! Then her head began to nod. She sat up straight, but her eyes shut and she tipped over against her mother, sound asleep.

Konok's mother sewed steadily on. The rest of the family went to bed, but before Grandmother lay down, she brought some reindeer hair with which to stuff the ball.

Ivory dog

An hour went by with Mother sewing as fast as she could. Another hour passed. Then Mother was stuffing the big ball just as full as she could with the reindeer hair. She sewed up the last seam.

"Konok, wake up," her mother said. She had to gently shake the girl to wake her. "See, Neeluk's new ball is finished." But when Konok saw the

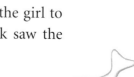

49

pretty finished ball, she was so sleepy that all she could do was smile. She would have gone to sleep again, but her mother roused her and helped her up onto the sleeping shelf.

"Will you be sure," Konok asked, "to put the ball where Neeluk will see it as soon as he wakes up?"

"Yes," her mother said, and she placed the ball close by Neeluk.

The next morning, as soon as Neeluk opened his eyes, he saw the ball beside him. He picked it up. "What ball is this, Mother?" he asked, leaning over the sleeping shelf to show it to her as she sat on the floor below him, working. "It is such a fine ball, Mother," Neeluk said, "and so large and pretty."

"Ask Konok," his mother told him, and Neeluk woke his sister.

"It is your ball," Konok said. "Mother and I made it for you because the dog tore up your other one."

Neeluk was so delighted that his mother and sister were glad they had stayed up so late to make it.

"With such a good ball," Neeluk said, "I think I will win a race with Keok."

*Eskimo
ball*

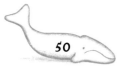

JANUARY

He carried Neeluk on his back.

Where Neeluk's New Boots Took Him

Your new boots are finished, Neeluk," said Mother as she took the last stitch in them. "Now you can put them on."

"They are fine boots," Neeluk said. The boot tops, made of hair seal, were shining silvery gray. The thin straps, with which Neeluk bound them snugly about his feet and ankles, were dyed red. When Neeluk stood up in his new boots, all the family admired them.

"With such fine boots," his father said, "you should be able to go hunting with me."

Neeluk did not know that his father was joking, and his eyes shone with pleasure. His folks thought it was because Neeluk was so pleased with his new boots.

Neeluk glanced at the new, white pullover jacket, called a "calico," that his mother had made for his father to wear when he went polar-bear hunting. Villagers called them "calicos" even though they weren't always made of calico fabric. Neeluk's father's calico was a long, loose, hooded jacket made of strong, white cloth. It was the same shape as his fur *atigi*, over which he would wear it. The villagers almost always wore calicos over their fur *atigis*. The women's and girls' calicos were made of pretty calico prints; but the men's and boys' were made of white cloth that was very strong. Sometimes they were blue in color, and Neeluk thought the blue ones were nicer.

Neeluk was glad his father was going to let him go bear hunting. He had never even let him go seal hunting with him. "It is not safe," he had said, when Neeluk had asked to go seal hunting. "We have to hunt on floating ice, and that is not safe even for grown-up men."

A light snow fell in the night. Neeluk woke up early. When he peered down from the high, wide, family bunk, he saw that his father and grandfather were gone, and so was his father's new white calico. They had gone bear hunting without him! Why hadn't they wakened him? For a moment Neeluk was sad and disappointed. Then he resolved to follow after his father and grandfather, running so fast that he would overtake them. He dressed as quickly as he could, new boots and all. His mother had gone to the storeroom off the passageway. Neeluk answered his grandmother's greeting and went out.

In the fresh snow outside the igloo, he could dimly see, in the half-darkness, his father's and grandfather's footprints. His one thought was to catch up with them. He did not know that the men had already been gone for a long time. No matter how fast he ran, he would never be able to overtake them. Neeluk followed the footprints up the beach and out over the shore ice. He was not going to lose his first chance to go bear hunting.

The ice became rougher. Neeluk had to walk more slowly. He had gone about two miles when the footprints disappeared. Neeluk looked in every direction, but there wasn't a sign of them. He did not know that he had come to the "drift ice," the floating ice that drifts with the winds and currents. Great level fields of it are often blown against the shore ice, where the drift ice may stay for many days, slowly moving northward, till an offshore wind drives it away. These great fields of ice are made up of smaller fields, and where they come together there are often dangerous cracks and patches of small, broken pieces of ice. The hunter must seek seals and bears among these cracks. The greatest danger for the villagers is that the wind may suddenly change and blow the drift ice out to sea, carrying the hunter on his great ice raft far, far from the safe shore ice.

Neeluk hoped to see the footprints farther on, so he walked right out onto the floating ice without knowing it. Soon it became very hard for him to walk.

In places he sank into the snow and ice almost to the tops of his new boots. Sometimes there were little drifts. But there were no footprints. Neeluk felt very lonely out there in the early dawn, so far from the village, but he struggled bravely on. To his great joy he sighted a speck in the distance and headed for it—for he was sure it was a man and hoped it was his father.

When at last he drew near, he saw that it was not his father but his uncle, Wemok's father. He was sitting near a crack with his back to Neeluk watching for a seal to come up for air. He was greatly startled by the boy's approach. He could hardly believe his eyes.

"*Aanikaa!*" he exclaimed in surprise. "How did you get here, Neeluk? On this dangerous ice! Who came with you?"

After Neeluk explained, his uncle said, "You poor boy! Your father and grandfather are far away. You cannot catch up with them. Come, I will take you safely back to shore ice. We must go quickly. Your mother will be looking for you." So he hurried and helped Neeluk over the rough places. When Neeluk's uncle saw that the boy was too tired to walk fast enough, he carried Neeluk on his back.

Small boy's boots

At his home in the village, it was a long time before Neeluk was missed. His grandmother thought his mother had seen him when he went through the hall passageway and knew where he was. But she had not seen him and thought he was still asleep. At last Konok woke up. "Where is Neeluk?" she asked. Then they thought he must have gone to Wemok's, and Konok started over there to see. Quickly she came back to say that Neeluk's footprints followed his father's and grandfather's to the beach.

Then his mother remembered what his father had jokingly said about Neeluk going bear hunting, and she started right out after him. She could see a long way down the beach, but no Neeluk. Then she began running because she knew that the men had planned to hunt white bears on the edge of the floating ice fields. Konok ran after her as fast as she could.

For two miles Neeluk's mother ran, till she came to the floating ice, where the big footprints stopped and the little footprints went on alone. She was sick at heart. Then she looked up, and there was Wemok's father coming straight toward her with something on his back, and, yes, it was Neeluk. How thankful she was!

"He is all right!" called the uncle.

When he set Neeluk down, he smiled and said, "He wanted to catch white bears." Then he hurried back over the floating ice fields so he would not lose a chance to get a seal.

Neeluk was so disappointed about not going bear hunting, and the walk had been so hard, that he could not quite keep the tears back. He did not understand why his mother was so happy. "If I had not lost their tracks," Neeluk almost sobbed, "I would have found them."

"The floating ice has carried their tracks far north by this time," his mother told him. "See, it has carried yours a little way. This floating ice keeps moving on and on."

But still Neeluk was sorry he was not on the ice with his father. His mother tried to comfort him.

"When you are a man," she said, "you can hunt white bears."

Boy's atigi

"If you had gone hunting with Father in that dark calico," Konok said, "the bears would have seen you far off. Don't you know that bear hunters must always wear white calicos to get within shot of a bear?"

Neeluk looked down at his once-white calico, now dark from months of wear.

"When the ships come in the spring," his mother said, "you shall have a new white calico."

"But if I cannot go bear hunting," said Neeluk, "I would rather have a blue one trimmed with red."

His mother laughed. "I will tell your father," she said, "and when the ships come in the spring, I am sure he will try to get you the kind you like. Now we must go, or Grandmother will be looking for us." She turned. "There she comes now!" she exclaimed. "And look! Others are coming, too, to help find our little bear hunter. Now after this, remember, son, that it takes more than new boots to make bear hunters of boys."

FEBRUARY

"Come and get a piece!" she called.

Wemok's Father Goes Bear Hunting

It was such a cold February morning that it would be no fun to play on the beach. "I am going over to Weeana's," said Konok, "and sew for my doll."

"I will go with you and play with Wemok," said Neeluk.

"Mother, may I take your pretty skin work bag to carry my things in?" Konok asked.

Konok's doll was a cute little toy, only about four inches tall and very slender. It had been carved from walrus-tusk ivory. It was a woman doll and had a nicely carved woman's face. Konok put it in her mother's bag, along with some little pieces of soft thin fur, a needle and thread, and a clumsy little walrus-skin thimble.

Soon Konok and Neeluk were on their way. They hurried over the snow and then crawled into their cousins' igloo. Weeana and Wemok were glad to see them. So were their mother and grandmother and great-grandmother, who were sitting on the floor by the oil lamps sewing fur clothes.

"Father has gone bear hunting," Wemok told them eagerly. "He and Keok's father went together. They started in the night."

"I hope they get a bear!" Neeluk exclaimed.

"So do I," said Konok, Weeana, and little Ahlook.

"I hope so, too," Grandmother said to them. "But we must remember that many men have been bear hunting this winter, and only two bears have been caught."

"I brought my sewing," Konok told Weeana.

"First," Wemok said, "let's play a game together," and he brought out some round bones, which they used to play a game like horseshoes, except that they sat on the floor.

"I can play, too, can't I?" asked Ahlook.

Ahlook was only four, but they let him play. It was such fun that they played a long time. Then Weeana and Konok sat down beside Weeana's mother while she deftly cut out the tiny garments the girls were going to sew.

The girls climbed up on the broad sleeping shelf to sew. It was nice up there. It was warmer, and the skylight was almost over their heads. Weeana and Konok had a great deal to talk about. As they sewed, making the tiniest stitches they could, they were talking together in low, soft voices.

It was soon midday, but Neeluk and Konok did not go home. They knew they would get nothing to eat if they went. Everyone was hungry, but Wemok's mother did not bring anything for them to eat either. It was a hungry time in the village. The men could not catch enough seals, and the meat cellars were nearly empty. They had to be careful with what was left. That was why none of the families in the village were eating a noon lunch.

Doll wearing woman's parka

"I wonder," said Wemok longingly, "if Father and Keok's father have caught a bear?"

"If they haven't yet," Neeluk said, "perhaps they are following the tracks of a great white bear and will soon catch up with him."

"If the men get a bear," Wemok told him comfortingly, "you shall have boiled bear meat to eat. We all want bear meat to eat."

The girls finished the tiny trousers they had made for their dolls.

"They fit well," said Weeana.

"Yes," agreed Konok, "and they are pretty, too."

"Great-grandmother," Weeana asked, when they came down from the sleeping shelf, "will you tell us stories?"

The five children sat on the floor close around Great-grandmother, and she told them stories they always loved to hear. Then they played together until it was time to go home.

"I do hope your father will get a polar bear," Neeluk told the other children longingly.

"I hope so, too," said Konok, as they backed out of the little doorway.

As they neared their igloo, Neeluk exclaimed, "The dogs are waiting as if they expected their supper. That means that Father and Grandfather must have come home from seal hunting."

"See," Konok said, "Father is just coming up out of the hall with the dogs' supper." Their supper was pieces of the poorest of the frozen meat.

The moment the six dogs saw Father with their supper, they sat down on their haunches in a semicircle on the snow. That is what Inupiat dogs were taught to do in those days. Father tossed a piece of frozen meat to the first dog. The dog greedily caught it in his mouth and then, in an instant, was standing on his feet, gnawing on the frozen piece of meat. Not another dog stirred to get it from him. Each dog waited his turn. Father tossed a piece to the second dog.

Neeluk and Konok were watching. Neeluk's dog, Ogluk, was at the other end of the semicircle.

"See," Neeluk said proudly, "Ogluk is waiting just as quietly as any of the older dogs."

"Yes," answered Konok, "but how eagerly and hungrily he watches Father's every move."

One by one the other dogs caught the food tossed to them. At last it was Ogluk's turn.

"See how well he caught his piece of meat!" Neeluk exclaimed as Ogluk ran a little way from the other dogs and ravenously gnawed on the frozen meat.

As the children crawled through the doorway of their igloo, Neeluk asked, "What have we for supper, Mother? I am hungry enough to eat a big seal." To his dismay, he saw that all they had was a piece of walrus meat, and not a very large piece either.

"Is this all?" exclaimed Neeluk, disappointed.

"That is all we can have," his mother answered kindly. She was very sorry when her family did not have enough to eat.

"Why can't we have dried salmon?"

"There is only a little left, son," she answered. "We must save it for times when there is no walrus meat to cook and there is nothing else to eat. Your father and grandfather have hunted for three days for a seal without being able to get one."

Neeluk looked at his father and grandfather. Since early morning they had been hunting seals in the bitter cold and had come home just before the children. They had taken off their boots and had hung them on the rack above one of the seal-oil lamps to dry. Neeluk knew his grandfather and father must be very hungry, though they did not complain. Neeluk said no more.

Neeluk's mother set the wooden dish of walrus meat on the floor and placed the bowl of seal oil beside it. "The meat will taste better," she said as she cut it into pieces, "if we dip it in seal oil."

Polar bear's tooth

Then the family sat down on the floor around the dishes and ate their scanty supper. Soon the meat dish was empty. Everyone was still hungry, but there was nothing else to eat. Neeluk did not feel very happy, but he did not talk about it.

Suddenly there was the sound of hurrying feet crunching the snow on the roof. Wemok's mother called down through the thin skylight that her husband had killed a polar bear.

"Come and get a piece!" she called.

Then she hurried on to shout the good news down into other homes, for that was what their people did in hungry times. When a hunter was fortunate enough to catch a bear or other meat, he and his family did not keep it all for themselves, but shared it with their hungry neighbors.

Quickly Neeluk's mother put on her warm *atigi*. Taking a wooden dish in which to carry home the piece of bear meat, she hurried out. How glad everybody was!

Neeluk's grandmother rebuilt the fire on the floor of the smoky kitchen. The kitchen was a little room with a sand floor that opened off the passageway. When the family needed to cook more meat than they could cook over the lamps, they made a driftwood fire in this room. There was a hole in the roof for the smoke to go out and the light to come in. Grandmother filled the kettle with snow to melt so there would be water to boil the bear meat in.

Soon Mother returned. Oh, how good that big piece of polar bear meat looked! Quickly it was boiling, and all the family were waiting, eagerly and hungrily, for it to be cooked. And when at last Mother brought the bear meat in and set it down upon the floor, how good it smelled! It didn't take the family long to gather around it. How good the bear meat tasted; everybody had enough. The family showered thanks and praises on Wemok's and Keok's fathers.

Neeluk's grandfather said, "Let us not forget how often the meat of a polar bear has supplied our wants during times of famine and tided us over until there was good weather for seal hunting."

Small, carved ivory bear

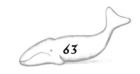

MARCH

Neeluk was not quite tall enough to look over the wall.

Neeluk Goes Fishing

I am going fishing," said Neeluk's mother one cold March morning. She dressed warmly, for it was very cold outdoors.

"I am going, too," said Konok. She did not mean she was going fishing, but that she was going to play on the ice with the other children while their mothers and older brothers and sisters fished through holes in the ice.

"I am going, too," said Neeluk as he wriggled into his two fur *atigis,* "and I am going to fish. May I, Mother?"

"You may, part of the time, if you want to," she answered. "But it is very cold lying on the ice. Fasten your belt tightly so the wind will not blow up under your *atigi.*"

The thick ice on the edge of the ocean reached a mile and a half out to sea. Near shore it was quite smooth, and boys and girls were playing on it. Not far from the children were what looked like many little, round snow forts. You would have thought the boys and girls had made them and then left them for a while to play at something else. But you would have guessed wrong.

Konok ran over the ice and joined the other children, but Neeluk walked on with his mother. When they came to the first round snow wall, Neeluk's mother stopped to talk with the woman who was fishing within. For inside every snow wall was a deep hole in the ice for fishing. The fishers had built the circular walls to shelter them from the piercing cold winds.

Neeluk was not quite tall enough to look over the wall and see the woman who was fishing inside. Neither could he see the fish—tomcod and little flounder, or sole—that the woman had caught and that were lying on the ice beside the hole. He waited patiently till his mother finished talking with the woman, and then they walked on, with Neeluk's mother sometimes stopping to talk with other fishers.

At last they came to their own fishing shelter and went in. The fishing hole in the thick ice was more than a foot across. The water did not come to the top of the hole. But there was no water in sight at all when Neeluk and his mother peered down the hole, for it had frozen over during the long, cold night.

The first thing Neeluk's mother did was to break up the new ice with a long-handled ice pick. Then she took her ice scoop—a little strainer-bottomed scoop with a long handle—and lifted out the broken ice. Next she placed the empty fish bag beside the hole to lie on while she fished. "Now watch me closely, Neeluk," she said, "and see just how I spear the fish."

Her fishing spear was made of spruce wood and ivory. Its spruce handle was six feet long and very slender, about the size of her little finger. At its lower end there were three sharp, barbed, ivory blades. But first, before spearing the fish, she must attract the fish to the hole.

As Neeluk's mother lay on the ice looking down into the water, she held a short stick in her left hand. Tied to it was a little string, and on the end of the string were some brightly colored jigging beads and bits of red from the legs of a bird called a guillemot. She moved the springy string up and down and back and forth, shading her eyes with her right hand so she could see better down into the clear water. Her spear was floating in the water, its long handle resting against the edge of the hole.

When a tomcod or flounder came to see if the bright objects moving in the water were good to eat, quick as a flash, before the fish knew what was happening, Neeluk's mother had caught up the spear and speared it. She laid the fish on the ice, and because the day was so cold, it froze hard within a few minutes.

"Mother," Neeluk asked after he had watched her awhile, "will you let me spear one now?"

Long-handled ice scoop

"Yes," she replied, and changed places with him. "Watch with sharp eyes, and keep the bright beads going just so . . . " and she moved Neeluk's arm up and down, back and forth, so he would get the right motion.

How Neeluk wanted to spear a fish! He watched closely. Ah! There was a tomcod—he'd spear him! He grabbed the spear and thrust it down. But he was not quick enough. The tomcod was gone. Neeluk was very disappointed. So was his mother. "It is too bad to lose it," she said. "If Father does not catch a seal today, we shall not have much of a supper except the fish we catch."

The fish were so small that it would take many of them to satisfy the six hungry people in Neeluk's family. Some of the flounder were no larger than Neeluk's mother's hand, and few were larger than his father's. The tomcod were very small, only five to seven inches long, with rather large heads and small bodies.

"Let me try again," begged Neeluk. He moved the beads patiently.

Suddenly a big flounder swam into sight. Down went the spear! When it came up, the flounder was on it. Neeluk had speared his first fish!

Neeluk was very happy. So was his mother—and she was proud of him, too.

"You must keep that fish by itself," she told Neeluk, "and show it to your father when he comes home. And because it

Flounder

is the first fish you have ever speared, you can have a party and invite some of your friends to come and share it with you."

As the number of fish on the ice grew, Neeluk longed to eat one right then. The villagers usually ate fish boiled or dried, but they also liked them uncooked and frozen.

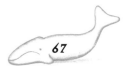

In the afternoon, as Neeluk and his friends played, Neeluk watched eagerly for his father. At last he saw him and another hunter coming along the beach, each dragging a seal behind him.

When his father turned toward their igloo, Neeluk ran to meet him. He held up his frozen flounder, an unusual, flat fish with both eyes on the same side of its head.

"I speared it, Father!" he cried. "I speared it myself!"

His father was very pleased. "If you can do that now, Neeluk," he said, "you will be a great hunter when you grow up. As you grow older you will spear seals first, then walrus, and then whales."

Then Neeluk and the friends he had invited to honor him by helping him to eat the flounder went into the igloo to eat the party supper his mother was preparing for them.

Jigging beads

Fishing spears

APRIL

The men in the boats drew the enormous black whale
close up to the shore ice.

Brave Eskimo Men Go Whale Hunting

It was an April day, but the snow and ice still looked as they had in the winter. April was the month when whales, traveling northward, passed near enough to Neeluk's village for the men to go out to sea and hunt them. The Inupiat Eskimo men were very brave to try to catch these huge animals. They had to travel many miles in their skin boats and usually had only simple weapons such as harpoons for whale hunting. The villagers needed whales for food, but they were so hard to catch that some years the hunters did not get a single one. When that happened, there was not nearly enough food to eat. There would be many days when the boys and girls, and grown-ups, too, would be so hungry that they chewed little pieces of walrus skin so they would not mind their hunger so much.

You can imagine how eagerly the people left in the village watched, hoping to see the brave hunters coming home towing a whale. Like all the rest, the boys and girls who were playing on the beach had often looked out over the water that day. Now it was late afternoon.

"Come on," called one of the big boys, "let's coast on the river ice."

"Yes," said another boy, "let's coast. The hunters are not in sight. They may not come tonight."

The boys and girls liked to coast on the river ice. The river had overflowed before freezing, so the ice was very wide. The wind had swept the snow off the ice and blown it into high snow drifts beside the river. Now the big boys ran down the sloping snow banks and slid far over the ice, sometimes clear across it. The flat soles of their boots were good to slide on.

The girls watched them. How far the big boys could slide! Neeluk and the rest of the younger boys also watched admiringly. Neeluk wished he could slide as far as they did. He was trying to learn.

"We will coast, too," said Neeluk and Wemok and their friends, but the big boys said, "You are too small to slide with us. You would be in our way and might get hurt."

The girls had gone a little farther up the river to slide. They ran down the icy snow banks and slid far over the ice. Neeluk and his friends followed them. "We will coast, too," they said.

"You are too small," Konok and Weeana and some of the big girls told them. They spoke kindly, but they were very firm. "You would be in our way, and you might get hurt. If you want to coast, go farther up the river."

So Neeluk and the other little boys went farther up the river and began coasting. They could not slide as far out over the glassy ice as the big boys and girls could. They did not run as far up on the drifted snow banks to get a good start, either. But they had a great deal of fun.

Neeluk kept looking at the big boys to see if he was sliding just as they did. After a while he said to Wemok, "Watch me. See how far I will slide this time." He ran a long way up the sloping snow drifts. Then, turning, he ran quickly down and slid way out over the ice, the farthest he ever had. But suddenly, almost before he knew what was happening, his feet slid out in front of him, he fell backward, and the back of his head struck the ice with a hard blow. He saw stars.

The other little boys ran to him. Neeluk got up, smiling through the tears he could not keep back. Most of the boys laughed at him and teased him, but some called to his sister, "Konok! Konok! Neeluk is hurt! He fell and hurt his head."

Konok came running. "I told you, Neeluk," she chided him, "that you were too small to coast."

"But I slid like a big boy!" declared Neeluk. "See how far I have come."

Konok looked back at the snow bank. "You coasted a long way," she said. "I did not know you could coast so far. Soon you will go as far as the big boys."

"That is what I tried to do," said Neeluk.

As Konok ran back to rejoin the girls, Neeluk said to his friends, "I am going to try again. Watch me this time." He ran to the top of the snow slopes. Then he turned, ran swiftly down again, and slid way over the glassy ice, on and on, till he stopped, standing straight on his feet.

"*Aanikaa!*" exclaimed his friends admiringly.

Neeluk was very happy. He had coasted like a big boy. He glanced down the river, hoping that some of the big boys, or at least some of the girls, had seen him. To his surprise the big boys were gone—all but two of them, who were running out of sight. The girls were running, too. What did it mean? Neeluk and the little boys ran after them as fast as they could.

Soon they could see a woman standing on her house-top looking off to sea. Could it mean that the whaling boats were returning? And if they were, had they caught a whale? Excited, Neeluk raced home. His mother, grandmother, and Konok were standing on their house-top, too, with glad, glad faces, all looking off to sea. He ran up to join them.

"Boats are coming, Neeluk," said his mother. "See, with sails up! And they are towing a whale! Let's harness the dogs and go with the sled to the edge of the ice and meet them."

Quickly Neeluk's mother and grandmother put harnesses on four of the dogs while Neeluk harnessed his dog, Ogluk. Instead of the long traveling sled, his mother took the box-shaped hunting sled. To this she hitched the five dogs abreast, each dog being fastened to the sled by a short walrus-skin rope.

"Grandmother and you children may ride," said Neeluk's mother. There was a board for a seat across the top of the front of the sled. Grandmother sat on this, with her feet hanging down in front of the sled. The children climbed in behind her. The dogs started off at a run, eager to join the throng of people already starting out over the shore ice. Neeluk's mother ran along behind, holding on to the back of the sled to keep it from tipping when they went over bumpy places.

"Are you sure, Mother," Neeluk asked, "that we will get to the edge of the ice before the men get there with the whale?"

"Yes," she said. "With a great whale to tow, they will come slowly."

It seemed to the children that it took a long time to go the mile and a half to the edge of the ice. When they reached there, they saw that their mother was right. The five *umiaks,* or skin boats, that were towing the huge black whale were still some distance away.

"Look! How big the whale is!" said Konok.

"Yes," her mother replied, her voice hushed and thankful. "It does look big, and remember, there is much more of the whale below the surface of the water than we can see above it."

How the people rejoiced! How happy they were as they looked at the great whale! How much meat there would be for them! Most of the meat would be frozen in their deep, outdoor meat cellars to be eaten the next winter. How much blubber there would be! The oil from the blubber would keep their igloos warm in the freezing cold of winter. There would also be valuable whalebone to

Carved ivory whale

trade on whaling ships for cloth, guns, knives, traps, and many other things.

Finally the *umiaks* reached the ice where the people were standing. The ice there was so thick that it formed a bank four feet above the ocean. Then came the great moment as the men in the boats drew the enormous black whale close up to the shore ice. All gazed with joy, their hearts full, knowing how much good this whale would do them.

Neeluk was thinking about what his father had told him when he caught his first flounder. "As you grow older, Neeluk," his father had said, "you will spear seals first, then walrus, and then whales."

74

"Mother," Neeluk asked eagerly, "do you think when I am a man I will harpoon a whale as big as this one?"

"Yes," his mother answered proudly, "I think you will."

Neeluk looked at the happy men in the boats. By their dauntless courage and skill, and good fortune, they had captured this great whale. As Neeluk looked at the successful hunters, at the gigantic whale, and at the crowd of rejoicing people, he thrilled at the thought that someday he, too, would bring home a whale for his people.

MAY

"What do you think of the big walrus, Neeluk?"

The Catch of the Walrus Hunters

I t was May, the month to hunt walrus. "Father," Neeluk asked, "may Wemok and I go walrus hunting with you?

"No," answered his father. "It would not be safe. Little boys never go walrus hunting. It is too dangerous."

"But we want to see the walrus," said Neeluk.

"We have brought many home in our boats," his father said.

"They were not alive," said Neeluk, "and most of them were already cut up. We want to see live walrus swimming and diving and snorting through the water."

"A walrus-hunting boat is not a safe place for children," said his father, smiling. "You will see enough of walrus when you are old enough to paddle and spear and shoot."

One morning the wind changed, making it safe for the hunters to venture out on the great ocean in their light skin boats.

Grandfather's walrus-hunting *umiak* had already been pulled out to the edge of the ice. The men used cleverly made runners to help them pull it. They had taken four skins of the hair seal, with the hair left on for better traction, and blown them up like balloons. Two were fastened under each side of the boat like sled runners, and the big, forty-foot boat had been moved over the bumpy ice like a huge sled. At the water's edge, the *umiak* had been tied fast to blocks of ice so the wind could not blow it away. Other boats, too, were waiting to start.

It was an exciting morning for Neeluk and Wemok and their sisters. They joined the crowd of villagers who went with the walrus hunters to the edge of the ice. There they watched the hunters launch their boats on the deep-green sea. The women and children watched them, not saying a word, each silently wishing them a big catch. They needed walrus for meat, and walrus blubber for food, and for lighting and heating their igloos. Walrus skins were used for making boats, tents, and ropes.

"Look," said Weeana, "now they are putting up the sails."

"See how fast they are sailing away!" exclaimed Neeluk.

Farther and farther the hunters sailed over the great ocean till they were but specks in the distance. Soon they could not be seen at all. Many more boats of walrus hunters sailed away that day, seeking food for their families.

Two days of good hunting weather followed—two long days, for it was light all day and all night. On the third day Neeluk's mother said to him, "Keep a sharp lookout for the boats. They should be back today. When they come into sight, we will hitch the dogs to the sled and go out to the edge of the ice to meet them."

Many times that day Neeluk and Wemok looked in vain toward the sea. "If we go a little way up the mountain," Neeluk said, "we can see farther."

"Yes," Wemok replied, "let's go up the mountainside now."

When they had climbed some distance and looked out over the water, to their joy they could see little specks in the distance and knew they were the returning boats. Thrilled, they raced down the mountain. "They are coming! Boats are coming!" the boys cried.

Walrus tusk

The good news spread through the village. Slowly the specks grew larger till the people could see that three boats were coming, one a short distance ahead. Neeluk thought one of the boats would be his grandfather's because his had been one of the first to start. The boats were low in the water, meaning that each was probably carrying four or five cut-up walrus.

All the families of the village harnessed their dogs to sleds to haul the catch from the shore ice to the village. When they reached the edge of the ice, Neeluk and Wemok were delighted to see that the first boat was their grandfather's. They could tell by its sail. As they watched, they could see it was lagging in speed compared to the other two.

"Why don't they come faster, Mother?" Neeluk asked.

"It must mean," she explained, "that they are pulling a walrus behind the boat."

The boats drew nearer, and Neeluk's grand-father's remained in the lead, although the others had almost overtaken it. "Look, Mother!" Neeluk cried. "They are towing a walrus! See how big it is!"

As the boat came alongside the ice, they could see that the walrus was about twelve feet long.

"The men in grandfather's boat have done best of all!" exclaimed Wemok. But there was another surprise for the boys. While Wemok was still gazing at the walrus, Neeluk, who was looking over the contents of the boat, saw yet another walrus inside.

Small, carved walrus

The work of unloading the boats was done very quickly. The meat from each boat was divided equally into piles. There was a pile for each boat crew member and an extra pile for the man who owned the boat. The hungry dogs hitched to the dog sleds were struggling to get to the meat.

"I am going to help," said Wemok's mother. "You boys can take care of the dogs."

It was all the boys could do to keep the dogs, especially Ogluk, from getting at the walrus meat. Nearby, some of the men were cutting a slope in the ice, up which the walrus would be pulled from the sea. Soon it was finished, and the men began to drag the walrus out of the water. It was so big, it weighed a ton. All the boys and girls watched while the men pulled and tugged, and tugged and pulled, and drew the great animal out of the water, up the slope, and landed it safely on the snow-covered ice.

The children gathered closely around it. They studied the great walrus from end to end. Its hair was short and brown and sharp.

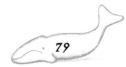

"See how long his tusks are!" exclaimed Neeluk.

"What a fierce-looking animal he is," said Keok as he joined them. "Look at his bristly whiskers."

"See how big and strong his flippers are," said Wemok.

"They have to be big and strong," said Keok, "or how could such a big animal move through the water?"

"Or squirm over the ice?" added Neeluk.

Most of the children left the big walrus to watch the unloading of the boats. Neeluk was so interested in the big walrus that he was still looking at it when his father came up beside him.

"What do you think of the big walrus, Neeluk?" his father asked.

"He is very big," said Neeluk, "and he looks strong and fierce."

"He was strong and fierce," said Neeluk's father. "It is hard work to catch these big walrus. It is dangerous, too. You see now why it is not safe to take little boys walrus hunting."

That night everyone in the village had boiled walrus meat for supper—and plenty more for meals to come.

JUNE

How eager the villagers were to reach the ship!